Into the Land
of the Lost

A Magical World Awaits You
Read

THE
SECRETS
OF
DROON

THE SECRETS OF DROON

Into the Land of the Lost

by Tony Abbott

Illustrated by Tim Jessell

A
LITTLE APPLE
PAPERBACK

SCHOLASTIC INC.
New York Toronto London Auckland Sydney
Mexico City New Delhi Hong Kong

Book design by Dawn Adelman

ISBN 0-439-18297-2

24 23 22 21 20 19 18 17 16   6 7 8 9/0

Printed in the U.S.A.   40
First Scholastic printing, April 2000

To William Durney,
first fan of Droon,
and a wizard forever

Contents

Into the Land
of the Lost

One

A Friend in Trouble

Eric Hinkle's best friends, Neal and Julie, had just come over. But when they entered the kitchen, they found Eric and his father crawling under the counter.

"Hey, Eric, why is your head under the sink?" Neal asked as Mr. Hinkle began hammering. Then he whispered, "Did you find a new entrance to you-know-where?"

Eric laughed and stood up. "No. My dad and I are fixing this leak." He pointed to an old pipe under the sink.

Blang! Bam! His father hit the pipe.

"I guess we can't go back to Droon till you're done," said Julie softly, so Mr. Hinkle wouldn't hear.

Eric smiled. Droon was the secret world he and his friends had discovered beneath his basement.

It was a magical place of wizards and strange creatures. One of the first people they had met there was a princess named Keeah. She had become their special friend.

Galen the wizard and Max, his assistant, helped Keeah battle Lord Sparr.

Sparr, of course, was the wickedest of wicked sorcerers. He was always trying to take over Droon. Now he was searching for something called the Golden Wasp.

Galen had told them the Wasp was an object of awesome magical power.

Good thing it was hidden. For now.

Ping! Bong! Mr. Hinkle kept on hammering.

"Look at this," Julie whispered, showing Eric a silver bracelet dangling on her wrist. "I bought a little fox for my charm bracelet. It reminds me of Batamogi."

"Cool!" Eric said. On their last adventure, a fox-eared king named Batamogi had crowned Julie a princess. That sort of thing happened in Droon.

Blam! Blam! Mr. Hinkle knocked the pipes even more loudly.

"I got new socks," Neal said. "Wanna see?"

"No!" said Julie, pinching her nose.

Neal pulled off his sneakers anyway. "Bright red. I call them my Ninn socks!"

The Ninns were Sparr's soldiers. They

were chubby and angry and their skin was bright red.

"Just don't lose your socks in Droon," Eric warned. "You know what Galen says. If we ever leave anything behind, something from Droon will come here. And something from here will go there."

Just then, Eric's dad stopped banging, stood up, and sighed. "I'm not quite sure what's wrong," he said.

Neal nudged Eric aside and stooped under the sink. "Turn that nozzle," he said, pointing. "You need to release the pressure or it will explode."

Mr. Hinkle frowned. "Are you sure?"

Neal nodded. "My dad does plumbing stuff all the time. That nozzle turns."

Mr. Hinkle tried it. "It won't budge. What am I doing wrong?"

"Listening to Neal," Julie said with a

chuckle. "Now put your sneakers back on, Neal."

"Yes, princess!" he said, scowling.

"Wait, I think it's moving —" Mr. Hinkle said. The nozzle squeaked — *err-err-err!* — then *POP!* It exploded under the sink. Water burst from the pipe and onto the kitchen floor.

"Wet socks!" Neal cried. "I hate wet socks!"

"The pipe broke!" Mr. Hinkle shouted. "Holy cow! We need a towel. Eric, get me a wrench! Everybody out of the way!"

The kids shot down to the basement for a wrench.

"There's water everywhere," Neal said. "Your mom's going to be really mad!"

"Neal, will you just —" Eric started, then he stopped. Julie was standing at the tool bench. Her eyes were wide with wonder.

And with fear.

In her hands was not a wrench, but the soccer ball that Keeah had cast a spell on. It was supposed to tell them when they were needed in Droon.

And now, across the surface of the ball words appeared in thin blue ink.

NOORD PLEH, EM PLEH, PSAW
NEDLOG EHT
SKEES RRAPS

"Eric-c-c-c!" sputtered his father from the kitchen above.

"We're looking for the wrench, Dad!" Eric called up.

Neal pulled his shoes on, took the ball, and quickly reversed the letters in his head. *Sparr seeks the Golden Wasp, help me, help Droon.*

"I knew it!" said Julie. "We'll help your

dad when we get back. But we have to help Keeah first! She's in big trouble!"

Eric nodded. Time ran differently in Droon. He knew they would be back before anyone missed them.

They shoved aside the large carton that blocked the door beneath the stairs. They jammed themselves inside a small closet. Julie shut the door. Eric flicked off the closet light.

Whoosh! Instantly, the floor vanished beneath them and they stood at the top of a long, shimmering staircase.

The magical staircase to the land of Droon.

Eric took the first step. Then another and another. His friends followed close behind.

The air was pink all around them.

At the bottom of the stairs was a rocky plain stretching for miles in every direction. Boulders lay scattered like pebbles tossed by a giant.

Eric wondered if maybe they had been.

"Welcome to the middle of nowhere," Julie said.

As the stairs faded into the pink air, a plume of dust rose from the horizon. The ground thundered with beating hooves.

"It's a pilka!" Julie cried out, pointing to a shaggy-haired beast with six legs galloping toward them. "It's Galen's pilka, Leep. And Keeah and Max are riding her! They're coming this way."

"So is he!" said Eric, pointing to a big flying lizard, diving down from the sky.

"A groggle!" Neal said. "This is not good."

The groggle swooped down at the pilka. On its back was a single rider, a man dressed in a long black cloak. Two purple fins stuck up behind his ears, and a row of spikes ran back from his high forehead. His eyes burned like fire.

"Uh-oh," said Julie. "It's . . . it's . . ."

". . . Lord Sparr!" Eric cried.

"Wet socks *and* Lord Sparr?" Neal groaned. "Already my day is ruined!"

Two

Under Sparr's Spell

Leep skidded to a halt and Keeah tumbled to the ground, out of breath.

"Sparr will stop at nothing," she gasped.

"And he has a terrible new weapon," said Max, Galen's spider-troll helper. His orange hair stood straight up. His big eyes blinked fearfully.

Kkkk! The sky crackled. Lord Sparr swooped down on them like a bird of prey.

"Princess Keeah!" Sparr snarled, leaping from his groggle and planting himself before her. "Tell me now! Where is my Golden Wasp?"

"She will never tell you!" Max cried fiercely.

"And you have to deal with us!" Eric shouted.

"Puny troublemakers," Sparr sneered. "Begone!"

Ka-blam! He scattered the friends with a bolt of fiery light from his fingertips.

Max was flung back across the dust like a bowling ball. When he stopped rolling, his eight legs were twisted and tied in a knot.

"My magic orb will make you speak!" Sparr said to Keeah. He pulled a black glass ball from his cloak and tossed it into the air. Strange designs were etched into the ball. It glowed as it hung over Keeah's head.

"Don't look at it!" Julie cried out.

"Ha!" snarled Sparr. "The more you try not to look, the more you *must* look. . . ."

He was right. Keeah tried to look away but could not. She stared into the orb's bright center.

"The Wasp . . ." she murmured, her voice strangely different, "lies hidden in . . ."

"Keeah, no!" Neal shouted. "Don't tell him —"

". . . Agrah-Voor," she whispered.

"Ah!" Sparr cried. "How fitting that I should *find* my Wasp in the Land of the *Lost*! Come, princess, let's go there together."

Sparr tore the floating orb out of the air.

"Oh, no you don't!" Eric shouted, leaping at him.

Kkkk! A sudden burst of light from the orb struck Eric in the face. The ball's crisscrossed jagged lines flashed brightly in his eyes. "Ah!" he cried, falling to the ground.

Sparr jumped up onto his groggle. "Princess, come!"

Without protesting, Keeah mounted the beast and sat behind him.

"We'll follow you!" Julie yelled, rushing to Eric.

Sparr's lips curled into a smile. "Such good friends. And now, a little fun!"

From another pocket in his cloak, Sparr pulled out a handful of wiggling things.

"What are those?" said Neal. "Worms? So, you brought your family along?"

Sparr scattered the worms on the ground. They grew long and thick and began to hiss. Soon the ground was swarming with them.

"Snakes, go forth!" Sparr boomed.

Hissing loudly, the snakes headed out across the plain.

Sparr grinned coldly. "Just a little some-thing to keep old Galen busy!"

The sorcerer pulled sharply on the reins and dug his heels into the groggle's sides. The beast left the ground. Princess Keeah clung to the sorcerer's saddle, her eyes blank.

A moment later, they were gone.

Julie helped Eric to his feet. "Are you okay?"

Eric rubbed his eyes. "I saw lines. Squiggly lines. That design on the ball burned into my eyes. Man, that hurt. The light blinded me."

"Ooh, that Sparr!" Max growled. "I'll teach him a lesson! Well, I would if Galen were here. Oh, I wish —"

Z-z-z-z! Suddenly, the air blurred, and a blue mist spun around them, streaked with blue light.

Z-z-z-zamm! A figure appeared before them, as the light continued to spin.

"Galen!" Julie exclaimed.

It was Galen, first wizard of Droon. He wore a long blue robe covered with stars and moons. His white beard trailed nearly to his waist. He was bending over, digging in his pockets.

"Master!" Max said, scrambling up to him. "It's bad. Sparr has —"

Galen stood up. "No need to tell me. Sparr has loosed his slithery snakes all across Droon. I must uncharm them one by one. That is why *you* must go to Agrah-Voor!"

"We're ready," said Eric, the pain in his eyes lessening. "Which way?"

"Not so fast," said the wizard, rummaging in his pockets again. "Agrah-Voor is the city of ghosts. It is the abode of the fallen heroes of Droon."

"So it's where the dead people live?" asked Neal.

"Just so," said Galen. "No living soul can harm another there. But there is a worse danger. You must be gone by midnight or all will be lost."

Eric noticed that the blue air continued to spin around as they talked. Were they . . . moving?

"What happens at midnight?" Julie asked.

The wizard frowned. "If midnight finds you in the city walls, you will become ghosts, too."

Neal gulped loud enough for everyone to hear. "Then . . . I think we'd better get started!"

Galen smiled. "Take this." He handed Neal a small hourglass. "It will tell you when to leave Agrah-Voor. The last grains will fall on the stroke of midnight."

Neal watched the tiny sand grains fall from the top of the glass to the bottom. No matter which way he turned the glass, the sand always ran in the same direction. "Now I know what they mean when they say that time is running out."

The air continued to spin around them as Galen pulled something else from his robes. "Take this, also," he said, handing Julie a small mirror in a silver frame. "Rub its surface when you need to speak with me. I, too, shall carry one. But you may use it only once."

"I'll take good care of it," said Julie, slipping the mirror into her pocket.

"What will Sparr do if he finds the Wasp?" Eric asked.

"The Golden Wasp controls the mind," the wizard said darkly. "It can make people forget. Turn them against their loved ones.

Change who they are forever. Sparr will become even more powerful."

To Eric, the wizard had never before seemed so serious nor looked so sad.

"Now," said Galen, "the quickest way to Agrah-Voor is across the Bridge of Mists. Even Sparr doesn't know this way yet. If you hurry, you can get there before him. And . . . here we are!"

Poof! The spinning blue air vanished.

Before them stood a stone bridge. Its near side was clearly visible. Its far side was shrouded in fog.

"Now go," said Galen. "I'm off to fight snakes!" An instant later — *zamm!* — the wizard was gone.

Eric looked at his friends. He could tell they were as scared as he was. Scared for themselves.

Scared for Princess Keeah.

Scared of ghosts.

"Let's do it," he said, trying to sound brave.

Julie, Neal, and Max nodded in agreement.

The thick mist poured around them as they stepped up onto the bridge.

Three

Bridge of Mists

"Now I know why they call Agrah-Voor the Land of the Lost," Neal said as the fog rolled over him. "You get lost just getting there!"

"Good one," said Eric, squinting to see him. "Everyone keep talking, so we don't lose each other."

Max scampered across Julie's feet. "I'm sorry about all of this," he said. "I should have protected Keeah much better. I'm not very good."

"Don't be silly," Julie replied, scruffing his orange hair. "It's not *your* fault. Sparr is a major sorcerer. Plus he's got that wicked black ball thingie. We'll find Keeah. Don't worry."

Soon the fog began to thin. Rocky walls surrounded them. Long pointy formations hung from a ceiling they couldn't see. Water splashed on the craggy stone floor.

"Somehow, we've gone underground," Eric whispered. "This is a cavern. A wet one. There's a picture like this in our science book."

"I smell something burning," said Max.

"That means people, right?" Eric said.

"Or maybe ghosts," Neal whispered.

A pale light shone from up ahead. Two

torches stuck out from the cavern wall, sputtering.

"We are not the first ones to travel this way," said Max. Then he stopped and pointed. "Look."

Beyond the torches was a short set of steps cut into the rock. The bottom step was underwater.

In the water was a boat.

"Wow!" said Julie. "It looks like something from a fairy tale! Or a dream."

The boat was painted yellow and blue, and each end curved up away from the water.

"If we're supposed to take that," Neal said, "it better float. My socks are just starting to dry."

Max clambered into the boat first. "There are no oars and no sail. I wonder how it moves."

When Julie stepped in, the odd little boat wobbled slightly, then became still.

Neal pulled the small hourglass from his pocket. "I guess we'd better hurry. These grains of sand aren't running any slower." He stepped in, too.

Slap. Slap. Eric turned to look back up the stairs. "Did you hear something?"

"Only my heartbeat," said Julie.

Eric stepped in. The moment he did, the boat pulled away from the dock. "Yikes! It's magic!"

"It's Droon," Neal said softly.

Eric gazed down at the black surface of the water. He wondered if it was cool or warm. He wondered if it even *was* water.

He dipped his hand in.

He gasped.

As his fingers touched the water, the

surface glistened for an instant, then turned crystal clear.

"I can see through it!" Julie exclaimed. "There's a . . . a . . ."

"A city!" Neal said.

It *was* a city. A tangle of odd buildings twisted up from the ground below. Eric could make out a high wall around them. "Is that Agrah-Voor?" he asked.

"Where the dead people live?" Neal added.

"It is the city of ghosts," Max chittered.

Suddenly, Eric's ears twitched. "Ninns! I heard them before. Now I'm sure of it. Ninns are coming!"

The next noise they heard was the sound of heavy feet slapping the stones.

"There they are!" Julie whispered as a band of fat red Ninns tramped down to the water.

"Augh! Small ones!" one cried out. "Stop!"

Thwang! Sploosh! A flaming arrow whizzed past the boat, splashed the water, bounced, and clattered against the stone bank on the far side.

"We cannot be captured!" Max urged. They all began to splash at the water.

"Both hands, Eric!" cried Neal. "If I become a ghost, my mom's really going to be mad!"

Thwang! Another Ninn arrow shot so close to Eric's ear, he could feel the flame's heat.

"I stop boat!" one Ninn grunted as he chased them along the bank. "I stop boat!"

"I have a better idea!" Julie yelled. "How about you just *stop*!"

But he shot his arrow, and it struck its mark.

Thwang! Crrrack! The arrow's tip struck

the hull just below the waterline. A thin stream of water spurted into the boat.

"A leak!" Max cried. "We've sprung a leak!"

"Neal, your socks," said Eric. "We need them to plug the hole!"

"My . . . *new* . . . socks⸮"

"No!" Julie cried. She pulled Eric's hands from the hole. "We need to sink so we can escape!"

"Oh, man, oh, man!" Neal groaned.

The small boat tipped forward as it took on more water.

The last thing anyone heard before the boat went down was Neal saying, "Glub! Glub!"

Four

Thief of Agrah-Voor

Silvery water rushed over the kids. Eric gulped for air as the boat went down. He hoped he could hold his breath for as long as it would take —

Suddenly — *whoosh!* — it was over and they were in air again. Flying *below* the water.

Cool air fluttered over them as the boat floated slowly toward the ground below. It seemed as if the boat were protected by invisible parachutes.

"Our clothes are dry," Julie said.

"Even my socks!" Neal said. "This is weird."

"This is Agrah-Voor," Max said.

Eric looked up. The river they had just passed through was like a thin stripe across the sky. Above that was the cavern and the Ninns peering down from it.

"Look at them," Max chirped happily. "Staring at us like numbskulls, tugging their chins!"

It was good to hear Max laugh, Eric thought. Even though he knew Max was worried about Keeah. And about Sparr and the Golden Wasp.

And it wouldn't be long before the Ninns stopped staring and started following.

The boat floated down and thudded

gently on the ground outside the giant city wall. They climbed out. The ground was hard and dusty.

"We did it," said Julie. "We actually got here."

"But we're on the wrong side of the wall," said Neal. "How are we going to get in?"

Before anyone could answer — *swoosh!* — something flashed down the wall at them.

A figure dressed in green, swinging on a rope.

"Aeee!" cried the creature, crashing into the kids. Neal and Eric tumbled backward over Max. Julie went spinning to the ground.

"Hey! He stole my mirror!" Julie cried. She sprang up at him, but he twisted away and scrambled back up the rope. "Rope, up!" he said.

"Stop him!" Julie yelped.

With one strong leap, Max jumped to the rope and pushed the creature off. Neal tackled him as he tried to jump away. Eric pounced and pinned the creature's arms firmly to the ground.

"I give up! You win!" came a high-pitched squeal.

The creature had a face something like a rat's, with a long pointed snout and whiskers. His arms were long and muscular, his legs bowed and short like a monkey's. He was dressed in a silky green tunic and wore a leather pack on his shoulder. His slippers curled up at the ends.

When the kids released him, he jumped to his feet and bowed. "Allow me to introduce myself. I am Shago, chief thief of Agrah-Voor. My fingers were made for grabbing, my arms for —"

"Just give it back!" Julie demanded,

setting her face in a fierce scowl and holding out her hand. "That's Galen's mirror. And if he finds out —"

"Galen!" Shago's whiskers curled sharply. "Oh! First wizard of Droon? Oh! Why didn't you say so?" He smiled so widely his ears wiggled. Tugging the mirror from his leather sack, he handed it back to Julie. "Queen Hazad speaks of Galen often. Oh! He is one of the great heroes of Droon!"

"Galen sent us here to help Princess Keeah," Eric said. "Who is Queen Hazad?"

Shago snorted. "None other than the ruler of Agrah-Voor! Come. I will take you to her —"

Splash! The silvery water above broke open suddenly. Ninn soldiers were jumping into the river and splashing through it into the sky, just as the kids had done.

"The Ninns are following us," Julie said. "We'd better move it! Fast!"

Shago snorted again as he tugged sharply on his rope. "Fat Ninns. They'll make craters when they land! Come, then. Follow! Follow!"

Shago's voice squeaked when he grew excited. But beneath his whiskers was a smile Eric liked.

"Follow!" Shago repeated, racing to the great wall. "Unless you'd rather chat with Ninns?"

"If I have a choice," said Neal, scrambling after the thief, "I think we'll follow you. Fast!"

But he couldn't. None of them could.

For when Shago reached the foot of the wall, he mumbled some words, then slipped quietly, smoothly, and impossibly right through the thick stone wall.

"Holy crow!" Eric exclaimed, jerking to a stop. "I think we just met our first . . . ghost!"

Five

The Ghost Queen

"Ghost or not," said Julie, "Shago's the only one who can help us now! Shago! Come back!"

Flump! Boing! The Ninns bounced to the earth, jumped upright, then rushed at the kids.

"Oh, man!" Neal gasped. "Hey, Shago!"

The thief's face popped up above the wall. "Why didn't you follow me?" he called down.

"We're not ghosts!" Julie yelled up. "Yet!"

"But we soon will be," Eric said, "if you don't send down your rope!"

"Rope, down!" Shago's rope unwound down the wall and dropped at the kids' feet. The moment the kids touched it, it began to pull them up. Soon they were standing at the top of the wall.

"My magic rope!" Shago said, beaming. "I stole it from a witch. But you must not think I'm a ghost."

"But you walked right through that wall!" Neal said.

The thief chuckled. "I snitched a magician's spell book once. Learned a trick or two. No, no. Only heroes of battle live in Agrah-Voor."

"Then why are you here?" Julie asked.

Shago's tiny brown eyes grew moist.

"My family is here. They are the true ghosts."

Boom! Boom! The Ninns were pounding at the walls.

"We must tell the queen," said Shago. "Rope, down!" The rope tossed itself down into the city.

Eric couldn't believe the view as they descended. Agrah-Voor was a city of twisted turrets and crooked towers, of purple stones and dark banners, of winding alleys and narrow streets. At its center was an enormous fountain.

Julie pointed to a large wooden gate. "Is that the way out?" she asked.

Shago nodded. "The Gate of Life. When Droon is at peace again, the ghosts will leave through the gate. They will live again. Alas, it has been sealed for many years."

"Because of Lord Sparr?" said Julie.

Shago gritted his teeth. "The evil one himself."

They swung lower into a crisscross tangle of streets.

"How can you tell where you are?" Neal asked. "These streets go every which way."

Shago smiled back at him. "The pipes," he said, pointing to a spidery maze of water pipes running along the ground below. "The pipes lead from the outer wall to the fountain. At the fountain we shall find our queen!"

Neal nudged Eric. "Good thing there's not a leak in one of *those* pipes!"

"If there were, we wouldn't let you fix it," said Julie.

Shago twitched his whiskers, and the rope touched the ground.

They entered a broad paved yard the size of a football field. The fountain in the middle spouted crystal water. All around it were men and women and creatures of all kinds dressed in leather and armor of every color.

Some warriors hurled large rocks to one another. Others clanged old swords against rusted suits of armor, sending off sparks. Still others ran footraces around the edges of the square.

"The heroes of Droon!" Shago whispered. "Keeping in shape for when they live again."

"They don't look like ghosts to me," Neal said. "Pretty colorful. Are they really, you know . . ."

"They are dead," said Shago. "But they wake each day hoping that today Droon will be at peace. As the hours wear on, they lose their hope, their color, their life. By nightfall, you'll see. They'll be different."

With those mysterious words, Shago led them to a large wooden throne. Pillow-shaped purple Lumpies stood at attention on either side. On the throne sat an old woman.

"Queen Hazad," said Shago softly, bowing.

Queen Hazad was beautiful but very old. She wore a crown, but it did not sparkle like most crowns do. It was oddly shaped, as if it were made of thick branches of wood.

But the queen's cheeks were rosy, and she wore a bright orange gown.

"My cane, please," the queen said. An old spider troll scampered up with a carved stick.

"Welcome," the queen said, hobbling over to the kids. "I sense you do not bring good news. We do not often get visitors, you know."

Eric bowed. "Sorry," he said. "I'm Eric. These are my friends Julie, Neal, and Max. Sparr has captured Princess Keeah and is bringing her here. Galen sent us to help her — and to warn you about something else."

"Sparr knows the Golden Wasp is here," said Julie. "He's mad and he wants it back."

"So the Ninns are trying to bust down the wall," Neal added. "They sort of followed us."

The queen drew in a sharp breath. Her cheeks seemed to grow slightly paler. "Guards!"

The warriors jousting with the suits of armor hustled over. "My queen!" they said.

"Gather my people," the queen said. "Agrah-Voor is under attack." The guards raced off.

The queen turned to the kids. "Sparr

cannot harm you or Princess Keeah. But you cannot stay long."

"That's why we're here," said Eric. "And to keep Sparr from getting the Wasp."

"The Golden Wasp!" the queen said, as if remembering something painful from the distant past. "It is a cursed thing with a sting that can turn love to hate, beauty to ugliness, life to death."

The kids shivered as she described the Wasp.

"Long ago, Galen charmed it and hid it," the queen went on, "but its power could not remain hidden for long. Sparr battled me for the Wasp. I kept him from it but lost my life. I took the Wasp with me when I came here. For so many years it has remained a secret."

Ka-blam! Lightning flashed across the sky.

"Until now," said Julie.

"Sparr has broken the wall!" a guard reported.

As the man spoke, more color left the old queen's cheeks. And not only her cheeks. The bright robes she wore seemed to turn gray, the color of ashes.

As Ninns thundered through the streets, other warriors began to turn pale, too.

Eric shivered with fear. He knew what that meant. Their hope was leaving them.

"Oh! Oh!" Shago cried nervously. "I am a thief, not a warrior. I must hide!" He scampered away quickly.

An instant later, the square was swarming with Ninns. Lord Sparr swept in with them. Keeah was held by two Ninns. She was still in a trance.

"Where is the Golden Wasp?" Sparr demanded, the fins behind his ears flaring red. "Tell me, Queen Hazad, or I shall tear your city apart!"

"I shall never tell you!" the queen replied.

"Then Princess Keeah herself shall become a ghost!"

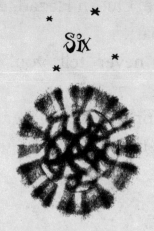

Six

Walls of Terror

The sorcerer roughly pulled Keeah to the center of the square.

As the princess stood there, silent, un-moving, Sparr pulled the black orb from his cloak and tossed it in the air above her.

"What is he doing now?" Max whis-pered.

"I don't know." Eric still felt the pain in his head where the orb had struck him with its light. "But I am really getting to not like that thing."

Eric stepped forward. "Sparr, let Keeah go! You can't harm her here, so why even try?"

"Yeah," Neal snarled, moving up behind Eric. "Why not crawl back where you came from?"

The sorcerer turned slowly. The fins behind his ears became black with anger. "You will not talk so bravely when I march into your Upper World to fulfill my mission!"

Mission? thought Eric. *What mission?*

Sparr then pointed his fingers at the hovering ball and muttered some words under his breath.

"Leave our princess alone, Sparr!" the queen shouted.

Sparr's eyes flashed. "Oh, yes! I'll leave

your princess alone. She'll be all alone. In-side!"

"Inside what?" Eric demanded.

"Inside . . . this!"

With that, the ball flooded its light around Keeah.

Suddenly — *fwang!* A wall burst up from the ground behind the princess. It was ten feet high and jagged across the top.

Sparr laughed. "Keeah . . . awake!"

The princess blinked, then looked around her. "Where am I?"

"In your new home!" Sparr replied. "Orb . . . continue!"

Fwang! A second wall burst up next to her. Another shot up on the other side. A fourth wall in front closed her off.

"Stop!" said the queen.

But the walls kept coming.

Some walls curved in, some bent out,

but all of them twisted and tangled around Keeah until she was entirely hidden by them.

"A maze!" Julie gasped. "Sparr is building a maze. Keeah will never find her way out!"

Fwang! As the last jagged wall jolted into place, the square fell into silence. The maze was complete. Its walls filled the square.

Sparr laughed. "I may not be able to harm your princess. But there is only one path through this maze. Only the orb knows what it is. It will take her days to find it. Weeks, maybe. Perhaps never! If your princess ever stumbles out, she will be . . . a ghost!"

"We'll get her out!" Julie said firmly. "You can't stop us!"

Sparr's lips curled into a nasty smile. "I

have no intention of stopping you. You'll stay to help your friend. And you will become ghosts, too! Ha-ha! I can see you getting pale already!"

His fat soldiers gargled with laughter.

Then the sorcerer whirled around. "With these troublemaking children out of the way, I am free to find my Wasp. Ninns! Tear this city apart! Queen Hazad, you will wish you had given me what I seek."

At Sparr's command, the Ninns began breaking everything in sight, trying to find the hidden Wasp. The ghosts tried to stop them, but the Ninns tore fiercely through the streets beyond the square.

The children stood alone before the maze.

"Keeah-eeah-eeah!" Julie shouted, her voice echoing inside the black walls.

The sounds of fighting echoed in their

ears, too. Max began to whimper as he paced in front of the maze. "What to do? What to do?"

Eric felt his spirits sink. Without even checking Galen's hourglass, he knew. There was no way to get Keeah out in time. Sparr would find the Wasp and become even more powerful. And their friend would be stuck in the Land of the Lost forever.

And yet, something about the huge maze seemed . . . familiar to Eric.

How could that be?

The maze was huge. Sparr said there was only one way to the center, but no one knew the way.

No one.

No one?

Seven

In the Mind's Eye

As Eric stared at the maze before him, he was sure he had seen it before.

"That's impossible," he said out loud.

"No kidding it's impossible," said Neal, checking the wizard's hourglass. "We'll never find her in time. Prepare to be ghosts, people. My mom's going to be really mad now!"

"No," said Eric. "I mean, I've seen this maze before, but I couldn't have."

Eric's head began to ache. It was the same pain he had felt when the glass ball shot him with its light. It still hurt. . . .

It still hurt.

"Oh, my gosh!" he gasped. "The lines! The squiggly lines when the orb's light blasted me. The design on the ball is the same as the maze!"

Julie blinked. "Do you *know* the way in?"

Eric closed his eyes. He suddenly felt helpless. And dumb. "I see some of the design, the crisscrossing walls, but not the whole thing."

"Galen could unlock your mind," Max said. "If he were here. But, of course, he's not —"

Julie nearly jumped. "The mirror! We can call Galen!" She pulled the wizard's magic mirror from her pocket and quickly rubbed the surface.

Galen's face appeared. "Ah! My friends. King Zello and I are keeping the spider trolls safe from Sparr's snakes. What news?"

"Sparr created a terrible maze from his evil orb," said Julie. "Keeah is locked inside."

"And Eric thinks he knows the way in," said Neal. "He's seen it before. Only he doesn't remember all of it."

"We must release his memory," said Max.

"Eric, come closer," the wizard said, waving his hand. A swirling light shone in the glass. "I will put you to sleep. When you awake, you will see the maze in your mind's eye."

"I'm ready," said Eric.

"You are sleepy," Galen droned softly. "Very sleepy. Your eyelids are getting heavy. Heavy."

Eric stared into the swirling light. His mind drifted. He felt sleepy.

He knew Galen was speaking to him, but he wasn't sure of the words. He felt as if he were falling. Then, all of a sudden, he bolted upright.

His eyes were open. The mirror was blank.

"Huh? What happened?" he said.

"I think you were hypnotized," said Julie. "Do you remember anything? Think, Eric. Think."

Eric closed his eyes. He tried to silence all the sounds. The distant swords clanging against one another. The grunting Ninns, the yelling ghosts.

If the sounds disappeared, maybe he could —

Enter.

He blinked. "Who said that?"

Neal gave him a look. "Said what? You're the only one talking."

Enter. Then go left three paces.

Eric entered the maze.

Neal turned to Max. "Maybe you should weave a spider-silk thread as we go. So we can find the entrance again."

Max's eyes brightened. "Good plan, Neal."

He shrugged. "I get one, every now and then."

"Three paces left," said Eric. "Then turn —"

Right, left, straight, left, back again, two rights, a sharp zigzag. It seemed to take hours to thread their way between the jagged black walls.

But Eric did not make a false move. Every turn, every angle, every crisscrossed line of the orb stood out clearly in his mind.

Then, finally, they took one sharp right turn and came face-to-face with a blank wall.

"What?" he said. He closed his eyes again.

He saw the wall there, too.

What happened? What was going on?

"No pressure or anything," said Neal. "But we're losing time here."

Eric put his hands on the wall. It was cold. Night was falling in Agrah-Voor. Soon after that it would be midnight. He suddenly felt very afraid. Afraid that Keeah would be trapped. Afraid that he had taken them the wrong way. Afraid that they would become ghosts — and it would be all his fault.

"This isn't right," he murmured, swallowing his fear. He retraced his steps. "Back up. . . ."

Julie shot a fearful look at Max as they

backed into a small space. "This isn't the way we came."

"Uh-oh," Neal mumbled. "Wrong turn."

"Quiet!" Eric studied the lines burned into his memory. No, he wasn't wrong. He wasn't.

He traced his way back to the wall again. He pressed against it. It began to move.

"Keeah?" he whispered.

Then, there she was, falling into them. The wall slid away as Eric spoke her name.

"Eric! Julie! Neal! Max!" she cried, nearly weeping with joy.

Max bounced up and down. "My princess!"

The sounds of battle thundered around them.

"Party later, people," said Julie. "Sparr is still hunting for his dumb Wasp. The ghosts need us."

Keeah trembled. Then she narrowed her eyes in defiance. "We must stop him!"

They followed Max's silken thread out of the maze. The sounds of fighting drew them farther and farther into the tangle of streets.

Many buildings lay in ruins.

"Oh, woe!" cried a ghost, stumbling past them.

Eric recognized him as one of the warriors tossing rocks earlier. Now he could barely support his own weight. It was as if smoke had taken shape as a person.

"The heroes have lost hope," said Eric. "Just like Shago said. By the end of the day they really are no more than ghosts."

"They're afraid they'll be in Agrah-Voor forever," Julie added.

"They won't be," said Keeah, "if I can help it."

Carefully, they entered a small square

surrounded by crooked towers. They dashed behind a pile of rubble and peeked over the top.

The ghosts and Ninns had fought to a standstill. Now Lord Sparr towered over the old queen.

"We are destroying your city stone by stone," Sparr snarled. "But now I believe that one of *you* is hiding my Golden Wasp. If you won't surrender it, you shall all perish!"

"You know no living soul can harm us!" the queen said.

The sorcerer cackled. "No *living* soul . . . yes. I've thought of that. Ninns! Bring in the box!"

Eric turned to Keeah. "Is that a new weapon? A box? Filled with what?"

"Probably not chocolate," said Neal.

Six Ninns dragged in a large black box. Their faces grew even redder as they huffed and puffed with the effort. Finally, they dropped it with a thud, tugged off the top, then scattered fearfully.

"What's inside?" Julie asked.

On the box was strange old writing.

"Oh, no!" Keeah gasped. "I hope it's not . . ."

"I'm afraid it is," Max whimpered softly when he saw. "The Warriors of the Skorth!"

Eight

Warriors of the Skorth

"Arise, O Skorth!" Sparr boomed over the box. Then he began to mumble strange words, as if he were casting a spell.

Suddenly, there came a scraping, clacking sound from inside the box. Then something jumped out. It clattered to the ground.

"Holy crow!" Eric gasped. "A . . . bone!"

Then another bone flew out. Then another and another. Soon the air was filled with bones jumping out of the box.

"Stop this, Sparr!" the queen demanded. Her ghostly people crowded around her.

The sorcerer ignored her.

"Arise!" he said again, and the loose bones began to form a skeleton.

Two feet assembled themselves. They attached to legs. A spine wobbled up, then two arms flung themselves from the bone pile. Fingers clattered into place. Finally, a skull flew up and sat on the neck.

The whole thing wiggled once, clacked its jaws, and stood at attention. Sparr laughed.

"I really don't like when he laughs," Neal said. "Because it's usually not so funny."

"It's not funny this time, either," said Keeah. "We need to do something."

"Definitely," Eric said, gulping. "But what?"

Eight more skeleton warriors flew up just as the first had done. Then they pulled armor and weapons from the box.

Some Skorth wore thick armor. Others were bareheaded, showing their bony skulls, their grinning jaws. But all had spears with blades that whirled and spun wildly.

They stood awaiting Sparr's command.

"Living souls cannot harm you, dear queen?" Sparr said with a laugh. "Behold the Warriors of the Skorth! As dead as dead can be! From ancient times, their only purpose has been to destroy. If you won't surrender the Wasp to me, you will surrender it to them!"

With that, Sparr cast his black ball into the air.

Zzzz! As it hung there, the orb shed light down on the ghosts.

The queen and her soldiers shuddered once, then became still.

"Sparr is putting them in a trance," Keeah whispered. "Just as he did to me."

"That's enough!" Eric whispered. "These ghosts need to defend themselves. I'm gonna blast that evil baseball out of the park!"

"How?" asked Neal. "It's twenty feet high!"

Eric wasn't sure. As he thought, he caught sight of a dark shape moving among the Ninns. While Sparr continued to mumble over the Skorth, Shago was sneaking around, stealing things from the Ninns.

Eric grinned. "Shago! I knew he couldn't disappear. Not with so many things to snitch!"

"Yes," said Julie. "Rope . . . here!"

Instantly, the magic rope, which was still wound on Shago's shoulder, tugged him across the ground to where the kids were.

Floop! Shago fell down behind the mound.

"My friends! Look what I have! A Ninn bow!"

"Shago, we need your help," Eric said.

He grumbled. "I am a thief, not a hero."

"Here's your chance to be both," said Keeah.

"I've got a plan," Eric said. As he explained it, Shago's ears flicked with delight.

"I can do that!" he said. Then, looking both ways, he scampered out from behind the mound. A minute later, he came back with a thin carved stick. He gave it to Eric.

Julie blinked. "Is that Queen Hazad's cane?"

Shago grumbled. "There are a hundred Ninns here. It's all I could find."

The thief scampered off. So did Eric.

Sparr finished mumbling his magic words.

"Now, go, Skorth. Destroy every ghost if you have to. But find my Golden Wasp!"

Clack! Clack! The skeletons turned and marched toward the defenseless ghosts.

Sparr began to laugh. "This will be good —"

"You don't know what good is, Sparr!" Eric cried from the summit of one tower. "Shago?"

"Up here!" Shago stood atop another tower, the Ninn bow in his hands. "My family are ghosts because of you, Sparr! Now I'll return the favor!"

Thwang! His flaming arrow flew at Sparr. The sorcerer leaped out of the way.

Then Julie, Neal, Keeah, and Max started hurling stones at the Skorth.

Finally, Eric leaped from his tower, clutching the magic rope in one hand and the queen's cane in the other. "Rope! To that ball!" he cried.

As the rope carried him across the square, Eric took a swing at the glowing orb.

"He swings —" Julie shouted.

Crash! The orb shattered into a million pieces, shooting light everywhere.

"— and it's outta there!" Neal whooped.

The queen stirred. The ghosts raised their swords at the skeletons, ready to fight.

But the orb's final blast of light sizzled up and down the length of the queen's cane as Eric swung it.

"Ahh!" he screamed, dropping the cane.

"It burned me!" He slid from the rope and landed in the square, clutching his hand.

The Skorth advanced once more.

"Stop!" the sorcerer suddenly bellowed. The whole square fell into silence. The cane lay at Sparr's feet. "Can it be?" he said.

Sparr waved his hand over it. The cane turned gold and began to shrink. It sprouted wings. One end became a flat triangular head. The rest formed the stomach and legs . . . of a wasp.

A wasp six inches long.

A wasp made entirely of gold.

"My terrible power!" Sparr shouted. "It's you! I have you again!"

The Golden Wasp began to buzz and whine, its wings flicking and fluttering quickly. The sorcerer pulled an iron glove from his cloak. Before the wasp could fly away, Sparr clasped his gloved hand around it.

Suddenly, Shago yelled out, "You shall not have it!" He leaped down at Sparr, but the sorcerer flung him to the ground. Sparr snatched Shago's leather sack and plunged the Wasp into it.

"Skorth, destroy them. Destroy them all!" Sparr growled hoarsely, clutching the sack. "Come, my Ninns! Let us leave this place. Agrah-Voor is the Land of the Lost. Today — we have won!"

His Ninns followed, grunting and howling. In a moment, they were gone.

The ghosts stood in one line, the skeleton men in another. The Skorth clacked their bony jaws. Then they aimed their spinning spears — *whrrr!*

"I think they plan to kill us," Julie said, backing up.

"I suddenly have another plan!" Neal said.

"The one where we run real fast?" Eric asked.

"That's the one!" Neal said.

Nine

Against the Gate of Life

"Ghosts of Agrah-Voor, to battle!" cried Queen Hazad. "These children are the future of Droon!"

Whrrr! The Skorth lunged at the children, but the ghosts struck back, wielding the swords they'd used when they were alive. Even Queen Hazad grabbed a wooden club and swung it swiftly.

Clang! Boom! The sounds of fighting filled the city.

Eric felt his heart race to see the old men and women stride into battle.

"We fight for Droon!" one ghost woman yelled out, her hands grasping an ancient sword.

"For Droon!" the others shouted, as if it were their old battle cry.

"Quickly!" the queen shouted to the kids. "Shago, take them to the Gate of Life. We will try to hold off the Skorth and meet you there."

"Are you sure the gate will open?" Keeah asked.

"It is the only way!" the queen said. "Hurry!"

Without another word, the four kids and Max followed Shago into the nearest alley. The thief wove a zigzag path through the narrow streets.

Eric could tell he was following the water pipes out to the wall.

Soon, they came to a huge wooden drawbridge, nearly as tall as the wall itself.

"The Gate of Life," said Shago. "But the hinges froze and the chains rusted long ago."

"It's huge!" Julie said. "We'll never get it open. Not in a million years."

"How about in ten minutes؟" Neal asked, gazing at the wizard's miniature hourglass. "Because that's all we have before the sand runs out."

Clang! Whrrr! The sounds of battle flooded out of the narrow streets. A moment later, the Skorth charged out of an alley, grinning.

"Man, it's creepy when they smile," Neal said, backing away.

"I guess they like their job," said Julie.

The ghosts poured in, but the Skorth were fast. Eric turned to run, then tripped on a water pipe.

A Skorth warrior charged at him.

"Eric!" Keeah cried, rushing over. She pushed him away just in time.

Clang! Splursh! The spear's whirring blades struck one of the water pipes and burst it. A thin stream of crystal water trickled from the pipe out onto the stones. The Skorth pulled the spear away and prepared for another lunge at Eric.

"Bad move, skull guy!" Keeah yelped. She jumped behind the skeleton, while Neal and Julie raced in and rammed him from the side.

"Eeee!" the Skorth yelped as he tumbled over Julie and crashed to the stones.

Eric leaped away. "Thanks, guys!"

"Oh, man!" Neal said, sloshing in the puddle forming from the broken pipe. "I knew there would be more water. All day, it's been nothing but — *that's it*! Water! Eric, give me your socks!"

Eric blinked at him. "That's a weird request."

"GIVE ME YOUR SOCKS!" Neal cried.

Grumbling, Eric pulled off his socks and gave them to Neal, who pulled off his own red ones and stuffed them all into the broken pipe.

"The pressure is building up," said Neal. "I can feel the pipe starting to rumble. Wait till you see what happens next!"

The Skorth formed a line and charged them again.

"Everybody, scatter!" Neal shouted, holding the pipe out like a cannon. It rumbled and quaked. It trembled and quivered.

The Skorth clacked their jaws and spun their spears. They were almost on him. Neal waited.

He waited. He waited some more.

Then he tugged out the socks.

KA-SPLURSH! A powerful burst of water blasted the skeletons back.

Crash! Crunch! Clack! Skulls rolled off their necks. Toes and fingers clattered into the air. Arms and legs bounced to the cobblestones. Still the water blasted them, until the whole troop of skeletons clattered together in a heap of disconnected bones and skulls.

"The Skorth are finished!" the ghosts shouted, rushing up to the children.

Eric and his friends gasped. But it wasn't because they had defeated the Skorth. It was because of what was happening to the ghosts.

"They're . . . changing!" Julie muttered.

And they were.

As Queen Hazad hobbled over to the drawbridge, her robes suddenly shimmered

as bright as a flowery meadow. Color flowed back into her face and hands.

And not only the queen's. Every ghost's ashen skin turned hearty again. And their clothes went from gray to bright yellow, blue, and green.

"What's going on?" Neal asked.

"The day is over," said Eric, breathing heavily. "I thought —" He broke off.

A tear dripped down the queen's cheek as she laid her hand on Eric's shoulder. "The bravery you children have shown today has given us hope. We did not die in vain. Peace may come to Droon after all."

Keeah stepped forward. "We'll keep fighting until our world is free," she said.

Neal nudged Eric. "I hate to break up this party, but we have a problem."

"You mean besides our wet socks?" Eric said.

Neal held up the hourglass. There were only a few grains left in the top. "Our time is up."

Ten

Good-bye to Agrah-Voor!

"Heroes of Droon!" the queen cried. "Our hope gives us strength. Open the gate!"

The ghosts took hold of the chains and pulled on them. They were strong and hearty again. They pulled with all their might.

Errrk! The chains rattled free, the hinges squealed, and the great door lowered.

Whoom! It thudded to the ground. The

ghosts stood in awe of the opening, then gave a cheer.

"Hooray!" they boomed. "The Gate of Life is open!"

"You have given us the greatest gift," the queen said to the kids. "Thanks to you, peace may come to Droon. Thanks to you, we are lost no more. Now you must go — you cannot stay."

Eric couldn't say a word. He couldn't speak. He had a lump in his throat the size of a baseball. He wanted to cry. But they needed to go.

"Sparr has the Wasp," Keeah said.

"He does," Queen Hazad said, her cheeks becoming rosy. "It could not remain hidden forever. Yet today was a victory. Knowing there are fighters for peace like you, tonight the ghosts of Droon will sleep in hope."

"Come," said Max, scurrying onto the

drawbridge. "We must leave. Our lives are up there."

Eric nodded slowly. Together, they tramped across the bridge into the swirling fog.

Woomp! Shago swung down from the top of the wall and landed at their feet. "Julie, I believe this is yours."

He held out a bracelet with a charm on it.

"Oh, my gosh!" Julie said, glancing at her wrist. It was bare. "How did you get that?"

Shago grinned his whiskery grin as she took the bracelet from him and put it on. "I took it when we first met on the wall. You never knew."

"But I thought Sparr stole your bag?" she said.

"I stole this back when he wasn't looking. Neal, Eric, you'll need your socks."

Shago handed them to the boys. "Now I must go back. The people I love are here. They need me. And I need them."

Keeah smiled. "We'll see you again one day."

"Yes," he said. "When I follow my family into the light of Droon. Until then, farewell!"

In a flash, Shago swung back up to the top of the wall, where he stood with all the other heroes of Droon.

"For Droon!" they called down.

Whoom! The Gate of Life closed. The chains rattled for a few seconds, then became still.

"We'd better go," Eric said finally.

The fog thickened around them. They stepped carefully into it.

"I hear water," said Julie, peering down. "There's a pool here. I guess we jump in, right?"

"Of course," Neal groaned. "I mean, what would I actually *do* with dry socks?"

Keeah laughed. "Hold hands, everyone!"

Splash! As before, the instant they touched the surface, the water turned clear. A moment later, the five friends burst up through it and out onto a fresh green meadow full of colorful flowers.

Bright sunlight touched their faces.

Julie laughed. "We're out. We're alive!"

"You are indeed!" said a familiar voice.

It was Galen. He rode up on his pilka. "Welcome back to the world of the living."

"Master!" Max chirped, climbing onto Leep's back. "Did you send those snakes packing?"

Galen smiled. "We did. We won a small battle today."

Eric lowered his eyes. "We didn't do so well. Sparr got the Wasp."

Galen nodded. "The battle of Droon continues. Now come. The stairs are nearby. You must go."

Neal handed back the hourglass, and Julie gave the wizard his magic mirror.

Waving one last time to Keeah and Max, the three kids raced up the rainbow-colored stairs.

When they entered the small room at the top, they could see Keeah and Galen and Max riding off through the flowers.

Eric flicked on the ceiling light.

Whoosh! The stairs vanished and the floor appeared where the top step had been. The kids piled out of the room and into the basement. The clock on the wall told them it was the same time as when they had left.

"Eric!" Mr. Hinkle yelled from the kitchen.

"Uh-oh!" Julie gasped.

"No problem," said Eric. "The wrench is right here."

"That's not what I mean," Julie said.

"What *do* you mean?" asked Neal.

Julie stared at her wrist. "Remember the rule about not taking anything from Droon because then something from here will go there? And start a whole big mess of things going back and forth?"

Eric nodded slowly. "What about it?"

"Well, this bracelet," Julie said, pulling it off her wrist. "It isn't mine. I had a cute little fox charm on my bracelet. This is something else, some other kind of creature."

Neal breathed in sharply. He looked inside the bracelet. "Made in Droon? Uh-oh. . . ."

Eric swallowed his fear. "Back to Droon,

right away. You know what could hap-
pen —"

Thomp! Thomp! Footsteps tramped
heavily down the stairs. Eric froze as his father strode into the basement.

"Dad!"

Mr. Hinkle frowned. "It took *three*
of you to find a wrench? I need it to . . .
to . . . ?"

Eric's father stopped and looked at
his shoes. They were starting to disappear.
Then his legs went invisible. Then his
hands.

"Eric? What's . . . happening . . . to me?"

"Dad?" Eric mumbled. "Dad!"

A second later, his father was gone.

Neal turned white with fear. "Now
your mom's going to be *really* mad!"

Eric stared at the spot where his father
had vanished. "Guys . . . we'd better —"

Julie nodded. "I think so —"

"Like right now!" said Neal.

The three friends sprang to the room under the stairs . . . just as the charm on Julie's bracelet began to growl.

ABOUT THE AUTHOR

Tony Abbott is the author of more than thirty funny novels for young readers, including the popular *Danger Guys* books and *The Weird Zone* series. Since childhood he has been drawn to stories that challenge the imagination, and, like Eric, Julie, and Neal, he often dreamed of finding doors that open to other worlds. Now that he is older — though not quite as old as Galen Longbeard — he believes he may have found some of those doors. They are called books. Tony Abbott was born in Ohio and now lives with his wife and two daughters in Connecticut.

THE SECRETS OF DROON

A New Series by Tony Abbott

$2.99 US each!

Under the stairs,
a magical world awaits you!